ONCE A SHEPHERD

GLENDA MILLARD

illustrated by PHIL LESNIE

CANDLEWICK PRESS

Once there sang a carefree shepherd
in a field of emerald green.
He lullabied his cloud-white lambs
and gentlied off their fleece.

Once Tom's world was all at peace.

Once Tom Shepherd had a sweetheart
who had cheeks like cherry tarts.
He crowned her with forget-me-nots; she spun and wove his wool.

Once their happy hearts were full.

Once a lark piped from a steeple
when Tom Shepherd wed his bride.
Its song was sweet as peaches.
Cherry's gown was blossom-white.

Once all the world seemed right.

Once Tom's darling sewed a greatcoat,
and she buttoned it with brass.
She stitched each seam with tenderness and lined it with her love.

Once she prayed to
heaven above.

Once Tom fare-thee-welled his dear one,
and he stroked his unborn child.

He wept ten thousand footsteps while a million raindrops fell.

Once he marched right into hell.

Once a shepherd, now a soldier,
in his darling's hand-stitched coat—
Tom knelt to help an enemy and fell, no more to rise.

Once a stranger closed Tom's eyes.

Once the sounds of war grew distant,
and the stranger took his leave.
Past ruined towns and cities, past Tom's emerald field he strode.

Once to pay a debt he owed.

Once he told of deeds and daring,
and he softly spoke Tom's name
while Cherry hugged the ragged coat against her aching heart.

Once she ripped
its seams apart.

Once a mother darned and mended,
and she made a small, soft toy:
a new lamb from a torn coat for Tom Shepherd's baby boy.

Once the world was all at peace.

With fond memories and many thanks to Mary Clark (teacher–librarian)
and the Year 5 students of 2009 at Seymour College SA

G. M.

For Tuniz, who drew funny pictures next to me, and
for Chi Chi, who nobody's even met yet

P. L.

Text copyright © 2014 by Glenda Millard
Illustrations copyright © 2014 by Phil Lesnie

First U.S. edition 2014

Library of Congress Catalog Card Number 2013957278
ISBN 978-0-7636-7458-8

14 15 16 17 18 19 TLF 10 9 8 7 6 5 4 3 2 1

Printed in Dongguan, Guangdong, China

This book was typeset in Quaver Serif.
The illustrations were done in watercolor.

Candlewick Press
99 Dover Street
Somerville, Massachusetts 02144

visit us at www.candlewick.com